DELERE

This paperback edition first published in 2012 by Delere Press

First published in 2012 by Delere Press

Delere Press LLP
370G Alexandra Road #09-09
Singapore 159960
www.delerepress.com

Delere Press LLP Reg No. T11LL1061K

This book is published with the support of
Avital Ronell and the Trauma & Violence
Transdiciplinary Studies Programme at New York University

ISBN 978-981-07-4336-9

Requiem for the Factory

Photographs by Kenny Png
Text by Jeremy Fernando
Layout by Yanyun Chen
with an afterword by Lim Lee Ching

DELERE PRESS

區馨彩
謝美好

Char-Maine Tan and Tykhe Png

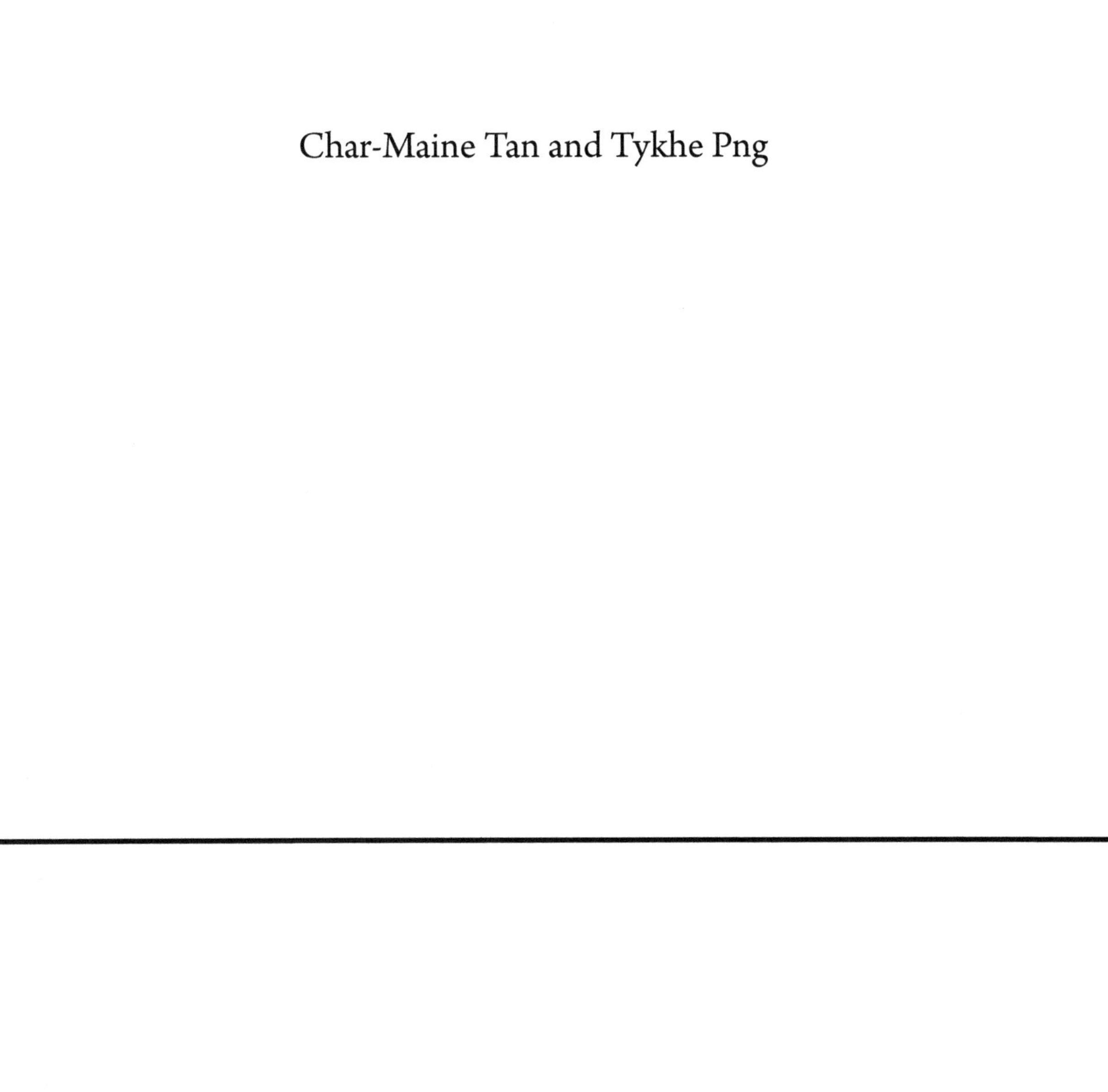

Chapter One

omething in me converses with himself.
Something in me converses with someone.
I do not hear them.

However, without me to separate them and
without this separation that I maintain
between them, they would not have each other.

(Maurice Blanchot: <u>Awaiting Oblivion.</u>*)*

And suddenly she felt that the end had begun.
Beginnings of the day had once
assured her that an end could come.

Once these assurances were gone—
perhaps they still remain, although
belonging to a time that is past, and
always already to come—her place in
these times, her space in time, was also lost.

Lost might be too strong a word;
especially for one such as her. But
certainly, it was already slipping
away.

Sometimes I wonder what the poster reminds her of.

Did she see it in red; was the red only for her?
Was there even a reason to see in red anymore?

She never struck me as one who saw in colour.

Would the red remind her of anything; would the red be
something I might have forgotten?
Though in this forgetting I must have remembered something;
in forgetting she has reminded me of something.

The last time she punched out, she felt it was her that was being clocked. No matter how much she disliked the place, it was hard not to become a part of it; in remembering her, it is impossible for her to not become a part of me.

Can you ever make a claim on something or someone—
can you say that it, she, he, is yours without you being a part of it?

No wonder she was uncomfortable seeing in colour; her concern was whether the colour would strip her of wonder, colour.

Would it not be more fascinating to take in the world completely devoid of colour—*tabula rasa*—where all shadings, tones, where the entire palate, are but possibilities?

工人以工为主
也要兼学军
也要学政治 学文化
军事 也要批判资产阶级
教育运动 也
批判资产阶级

Time used to bother her more than
anything else; after all, her space was fixed,
determined, set by a schedule, routine; time.

Punching out was her ticket to
freedom. How she longed to punch again—the trouble with
knocking down your opponent is
that they may not always rise.

She longed for another adversary;
something to pit herself against—learn its moves, strategies,
techniques; spar, train, hurl herself into constant battle.

This time she might have done too well

毛主席教导
工人以工为主
也要兼学军事、政治、文化
也要搞社会主义
教育运动，也要
批判资产阶级
教育

Or maybe, her opponent had one last trick up his sleeve—he disappeared.

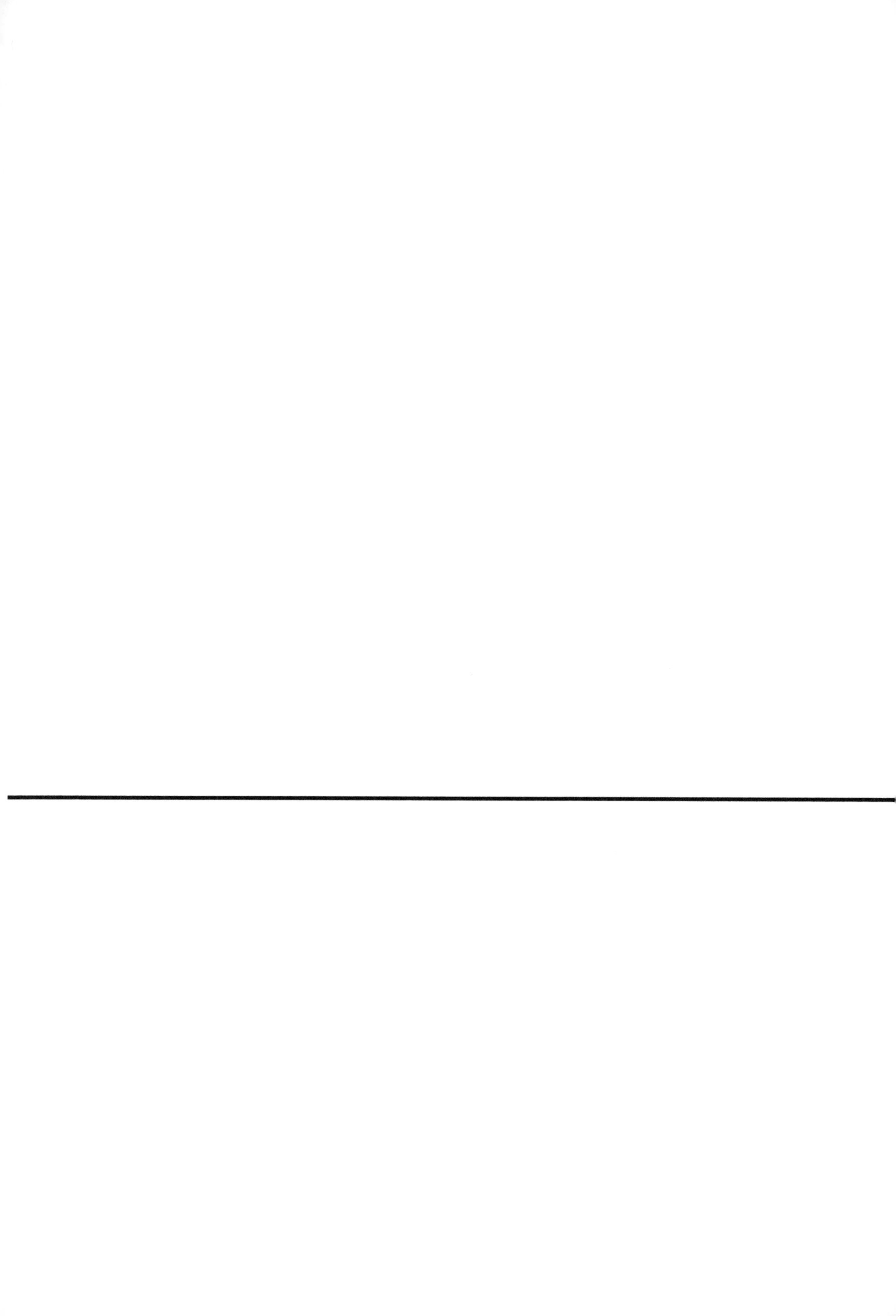

And now she had no one, nothing, to match up with, stand against.
Now that she had everything to match up, now that there was
no one she couldn't stand up to, the problem was: what to go up
against.

The punch had allowed her to momentarily taste victory—
by punching through him, she had also burst the walls of the
clock; broken through the confines of time itself.

No wonder she was seeing red
Without time, there is nothing to wait for
Without time, there is nothing to do but wait

Left without a daily experience of limited time—time itself—all
she had, all she could do—perhaps all we can ever do—was to
recall, to re-enter memory.

I suspect that at some point, she must have regretted not ever
having taken photographs.

I suspect that she always knew the futility of allowing light to write—not only would she have to put her hand into play, she also would have had to read what light had written.

In the end, all she would have seen is red

She often remembered that her only hope lay in forgetting. Not just of the time that was, or even of time itself, but the forgetting that memory itself brings.

Perhaps this is how hope works—
she long realised that one cannot hope for something unless one has already forgotten what that thing is.

In forgetting all hope lies

All hope in forgetting lies

I imagine she must have spent a lot of time walking around,
looking about, walking through. Whether she actually saw more
this time perhaps remains known only to her—something you
may be more privy to than I.

There was a time when she would have told me her thoughts, her
dreams, her memories—can someone tell you other than their
memories; when they tell you, does it become a future possibility?

That might have been the reason she used to tell me so much—
her distaste of time

毛主席说
工人以工为主，也要兼学军事、政治、文化，也要搞社会主义教育运动，也要批判资产阶级。

Can one even begin to posit why she tells me these tales—
can ever one do anything but posit.

Even I; especially I.

For, I know not why I have been called to witness her, be a witness
for her. Can one do so? Can one be a witness?

In this case one—I—cannot ever be sure what, or to—for—
whom, I am witnessing: all I can ever say, testify to, is the fact that
I am witnessing.

Occasionally, I wonder if this has something to do with the red ribbon she sees—that I think she sees. Perhaps as her witness, I am at times seeing for her; perhaps I see what she does not see, cannot see.

It is not that inconceivable that I see what is not there; if she did not see it, does it still matter?

Surely we are not bound by what we know—imagine the responsibility we would have if trees could not fall independently of us.

During her moments of free time, she wondered whose fate was
worse:

Sisyphus or Atlas—whenever he tired of hoisting the rock up
the mountain only to find himself back at the same place, was he
thankful that what he did mattered little, made no difference at all?

How she hated having time

Sometime I wonder about this call to witnessing—
how do, can, I know if the call I am hearing is the one that was sent
out, is the one that was sent in my direction?

Whenever one sends out a call, a post-card, one never knows
where it will end up, whether it will land.

When one picks up a call, one never knows where it comes from;
what if it were—they are—just voices in my head?

Maybe the red ribbon sees for us.

When we see something—call it into being by
witnessing to it—does it also see us; perhaps we only unveil
insofar as it allows the unveiling. Perhaps she only sees the ribbon
as there was nothing else to see.

Whilst looking at nothing, does the thing then allow itself to be
seen—by her sitting still, doing nothing.

In her absolute boredom, in her waiting for time itself, she let time
see her.

By seeing that she is nothing but in time.

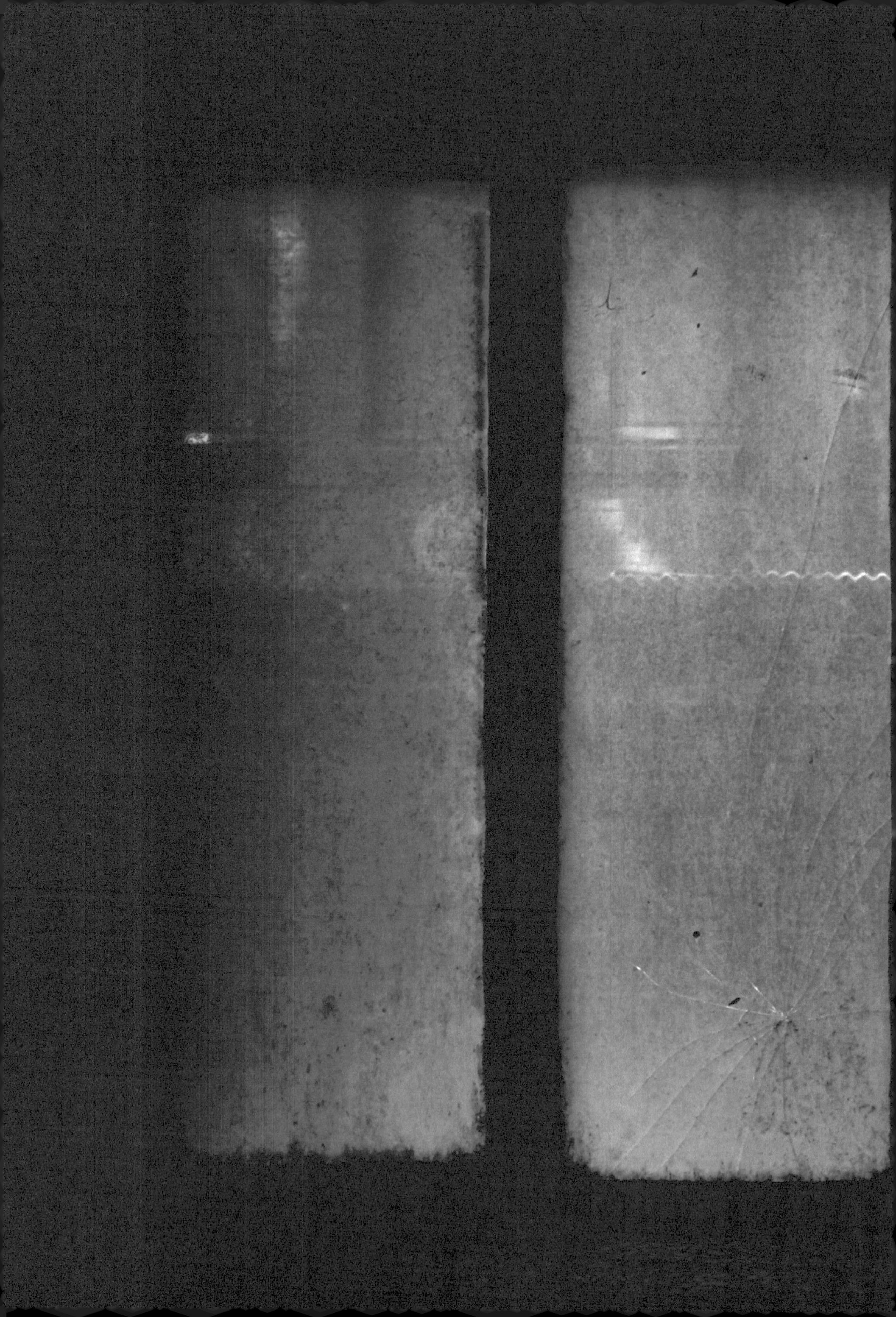

Sometimes she longed to tell someone a secret, the secret, that she often did not quite spend all her time at work in work. Even though one is there, one can always also be anywhere.

When she was younger, she would have been apprehensive about telling me.

But now she has realised that I would not have known—will never know; that it is a secret as long as she did not reveal that it were so.

Chapter Two

My mission is to kill time,
and time's to kill me in return.
How comfortable one is among murderers.

(the spectre of E.M Cioran; séance by Jean Baudrillard
and Enrique Noialles: <u>Exiles from Dialogue</u>.)

"Why should I wait for you?" she said—
his manner suggested he was not quite certain.

Was she referring to a particular need for a reason?
That he felt he could quite easily simulate.

Or, was she speaking of a notion of time.

After all, responding requires at least a certain amount of
correspondence.

"What do you mean?" he says, in a particular voice that
oscillates between question and statement, between asking and
commenting.

At that point she nods.
"Sometimes all you need do is utter."
---"Why would you think I was actually interested in what you
were saying?"

"But if you don't actually bother about what I say, why are you still
talking to me?"
--- "Is there anyone else to talk with?"
--- "Would it matter if it was someone else?"
--- "As long as it is somebody else."

Am I only drawn to you because there is something to be drawn
towards?

"Should I reach out and touch you?"

Just call me angel of the morning angel.
Just touch my cheeks before you leave me baby.

(Merrillee Rush: <u>Angel of the Morning</u>)

"If it doesn't matter whom you are talking with, should I just leave?"
---"No … stay"
---"Even if you don't say anything, just stay"
--- "Perhaps it is better if you don't say anything."

"Is it because I might offend you, contradict you; detach myself from you?"
---"No. It is only when one is silent that there is something to say."

Once said, all that is left is the unsayable.
One can only speak that which cannot be spoken.

"How then does one say '*I do*' to another?"
---"One doesn't. It's always already in front of one, written for one. All you have to do is read."

Literature waxes on tragedy as the true sign of love; death is its supreme indicator. One is supposed to die in order to prove one's love to the other.

Romeo & Juliet
Tristan & Isolde
Guinevere & Lancelot
Cleopatra & Anthony

4 great sets of lovers. 4 great tragedies.

But this is, of course, where most have missed the point. The death that is required is not one in the realm of the physical, but rather a death to other people, other possibilities.

The eternal in erotic love is that in its moment individuals first come into existence for each other.

(Søren Kierkegaard: <u>The Seducer's Diary.</u>*)*

And this is the moment of the *I do*; nothing more, and infinitely nothing less. The promise that is made about the future, which is always already in the past; and lived out in the present. For, the saying when *two become one* is never about people—that would be impossible—but about time. And in this moment lies a nod towards madness—how can one person possibly say, at any juncture, with any certainty, that (s)he will spend her life with this other person. But it is this moment of madness, this "I do," which translates to *I will spend the rest of my life with this person even though I know it is not possible to say it with any surety,* that gives marriage its beauty. It is this truly mad decision that saves marriage from banality; and allows us to catch a glimpse of the sublime.

"In fact, here, one is tempted to take it all the way, and posit that not only is it an act of madness, it is also an act of sheer stupidity; where one makes the decision with no reason, makes a decision that is beyond any reason."

"Isn't that true of any relationality?"

"Yes and no"

"After all, one cannot say that something is true when it has to be in place for relationality to even occur."

Chapter Three

What happens when one names another, when one draws them
into language—
is that the moment in which they disappear?; when they begin
slipping away, into nothingness.

Can I only begin to love you in your absence?

Do we otherwise end up in relative spaces with each other—
merely two characters in the same novel?

Only when we remain irreducibly singular—and yet in a
relationality with each other—is love even possible.

Perhaps only when the other remains nameless.

What if we begin with the premise that there is nothing to begin
with?

That might be the case when one first attempts to touch another;
if that touch has no *a priori* intent, no motive—
if that touch attempts to do nothing but touch.

But this is then a nothingness that is not of the order of absence, nor of a lack; this is a nothingness that wants for nothing, is nothing other than a full potentiality, is nothing but possibilities— whilst at the same time, in the same moment, within the same gesture, recognises the very potential not-to-be.

A not-to-be that is always already; but just not yet.

Otherwise, when she clocks out she would merely be without a factory.

However, it is not as if the factory ever leaves her—even as she may have left it. Even though she attempts to punch the factory out of her life, her self.

T
THE
OF
I
H
MY
WAS
REOCCUPATION
WAR
OCCUPATION
E
THE
TIMES
PRODUCT
A

THE
TO
I
REOCCUPATION
OCCUPATION
MUCH
WAS
PRODUCTION

Did the factory always factor in my desire of wanting to be
someone other than another of the ones in her realm;
not just one of those that clocked, docked, in and out; one that
resisted being exchangeable, mutable, the same.

We can only speculate whether she was ever able to do so.

What seems to make it even more impossible now is the difficulty
in hitting a spectre.

After all, we can only see ghosts when we are not looking—and it
would seem quite difficult to punch blindly.

That is unless she manages to see with her third eye: how she
becomes her own shaman though remains to be seen.

Perhaps we should allow ourselves a moment to posit.

There is a possibility that she can momentarily leave if she takes into account her own blindness. For, only by not seeing do we leave any space, possibility, for us to see.

And here, one must make no mistake: she will be held accountable for all of this.

Even if she cannot know what she may see, or even will see, even if she knows not what she does.

If she is blind, might she momentarily forget?

For, if seeing is believing, is blindness a turning away from knowing, from memory?—forgetting itself.

If one must be blind to see, then seeing itself is always already blind.

If she is always already blind, might her remembering not also remind us that all memory potentially brings with it forgetting.

Not that she can choose to forget—even as all hope lies in forgetting.

There is, of course, an irony in attempting to foreground an unknowability.

Absurd even.

But most of our hope lies in absurdity.

All potentiality is in the to-come; a to-come that we cannot rely on, cannot even know—a to-come that we may always already have forgotten.

A potentiality—a hope—that may lie to us.

What a beautiful lie it is too

Forgetting. Unknowability.
Exteriority. Finitude.

All names that name the fact that we cannot name.

All names for hope.

The names that remain nameless.

The names of the nameless.

THE

TO
F
E

I

MY   WAS

REOCCUPATION

H
OCCUPATION   PRODUC
                   TO
                   TIME
                   TOMUCH
NENESTA

Haec quotiescumque feceritis, in mei memoriam facietis.

Mysterium fidei.

Love

耐ヘ難キヲ耐ヘ忍ヒ難キヲ忍ヒ

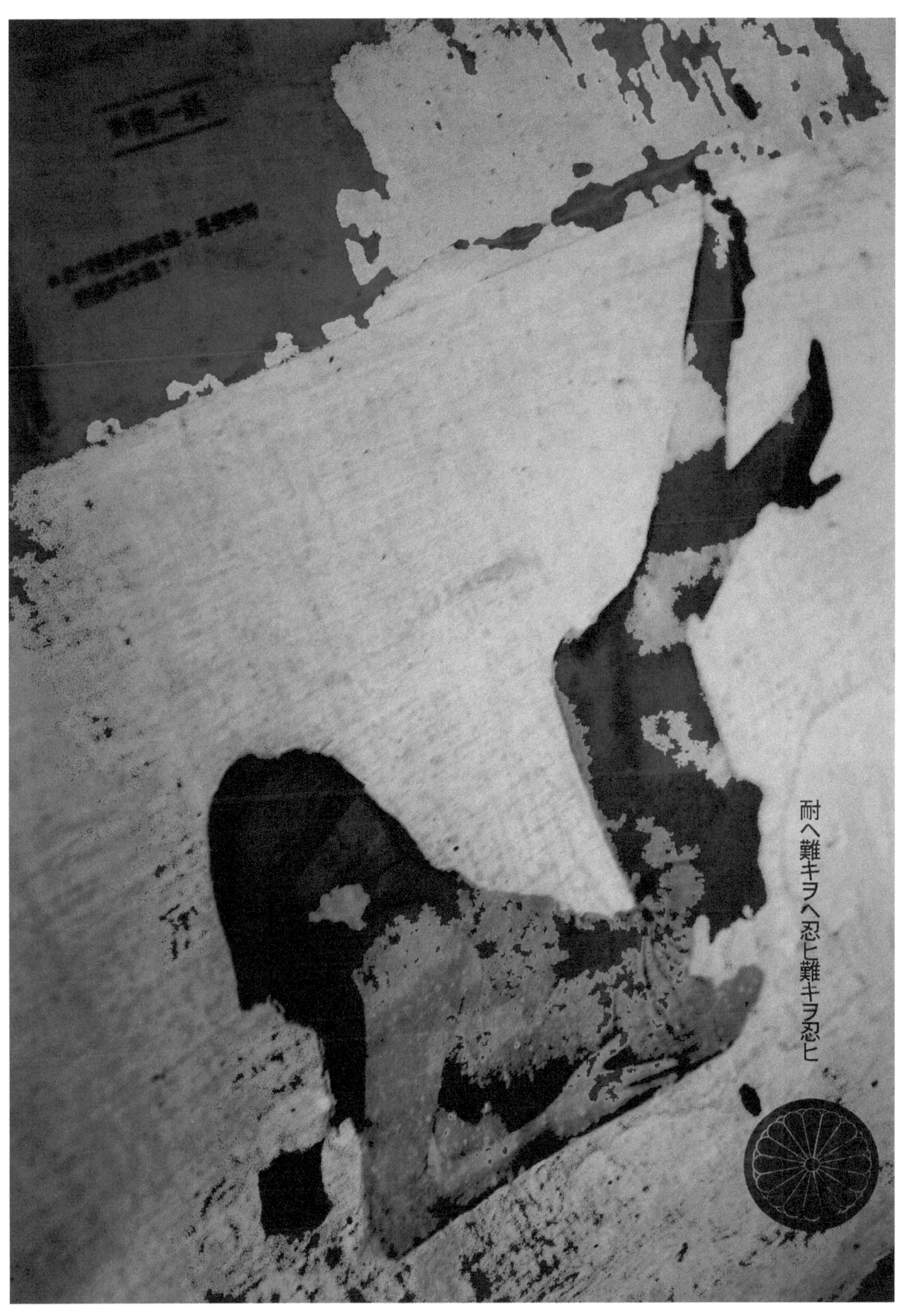
耐ヘ難キヲ忍ヒ難キヲ忍ヒ

雨ヘ難キヲヘ忍ヒ難キヲヲ忍ヒ

耐ヘ難キヲ耐ヘ忍ヒ難キヲ忍ヒ

耐ヘ難キヲ堪ヘ忍ヒ難キヲ忍ヒ

Chapter Four

On letters; or, a confession

It should have been easy—easier—to write this to you.

Perhaps it should have begun with "Dear you"—
after all, why would one write to someone unless they were—
you are—dear.

In fact, the question of *why do something unless driven by desire* is
one that lingers, remains; is a spectre behind every letter, post-
card, deed, writing.

Why do something unless you want to?
Mere mortals; forever forgetful of Death,
hitching a ride, leaning on the street lights
burning bright

A note found lying around.
Awaiting the moment to be read—
not as if we, I, you, will, can, ever quite know the right moment.

For, it is not like trust was, is, even a concern of the note, of her
note.

Or if she wrote it with you in mind; perhaps even she cannot know
that.

Since she, I, cannot know of whom—let alone why—I write,
the question will continue to haunt, to roam; refusing exorcism;
requiring—demanding—time.

In the anxiousness of writing this letter to you—in the anxiety
of wanting to know, being unable to know, who you are, who is
reading this—is the reification of time itself.

Time stops the moment I send this off; to you.

A moment that you can only see when—as—you read this; a
moment that you will never be able to see as you read this; a
moment that you will never be able to see even as you read this;
even if you were—are—able to read this.

All one can do—all I can do—is: send it off.
After which, all that is left is hope. Not just faith in where it lands,
but whether it even does. Even if it lands, does it ever do so? The
moment I send it off, I no longer even know—perhaps I never
did—where it was supposed to land.

Maybe there is no other way than to acknowledge the note—her
note—away from the note itself. I am reading blindly;

I am also always already writing this blind.

But dearly; for sure.

We might attempt to avoid the trope of expenses, the expensive—
valuation—and try to defer it for as long as possible,
but clearly we—I— have been unable to prevent its visitation.

Can one calculate time?

Or, even more absurdly,
put a value to it?

But isn't time money?

Or has money—and all value—been precisely an attempt to
concretise time?

After all, this was the only way I could have punched out; if they
were not paying for my time, I would have been stuck there—
forever.

All I ever had to do was give up my time; time that was not mine
to begin with.

For, the only way one can actually give up—away—something is if
it doesn't belong to one in the first place.

An echo in my mind—the constant reminder that there is *no time
to lose.*

A call to hurry, to do as much as I can in as little time as possible
… after all, the clock is always moving and all we are doing is
attempting to catch up.

But then, if there always was *no time,* then there was—is—nothing
to lose in the first place; the time that is lost, loss, that passes, was,
is, never mine, yours, hers, to lose to begin with.

Perhaps then, I was always paid—since *time is money*—for something that was never mine.

Perhaps, I was paid precisely to lose this time.

One does wonder if the ultimate loss of time—*lost in time*—is that
of memory itself?

In a sense, perhaps this payment is always already a remuneration
to forget—and one might even hear echoes of Nietzsche here,
where happiness is precisely the ability to forget.

What wouldn't we pay in order to forget…

Not that we even have the possibility of
determining what we forget—what wouldn't we give in order to
know what we forgot.

And if we are strictly speaking paying for nothing, it is a ritual.

Perhaps forgetting as such is always already symbolic—named
only because one has to name—naming something that cannot be
named.

Perhaps this is—has always been—the difficulty of writing a
letter; haunted by the fact that all we have are letters.

All we are doing is writing—all we can do is write—with something that disappears as it is seen, can only be seen as it disappears.

This is a writing of light

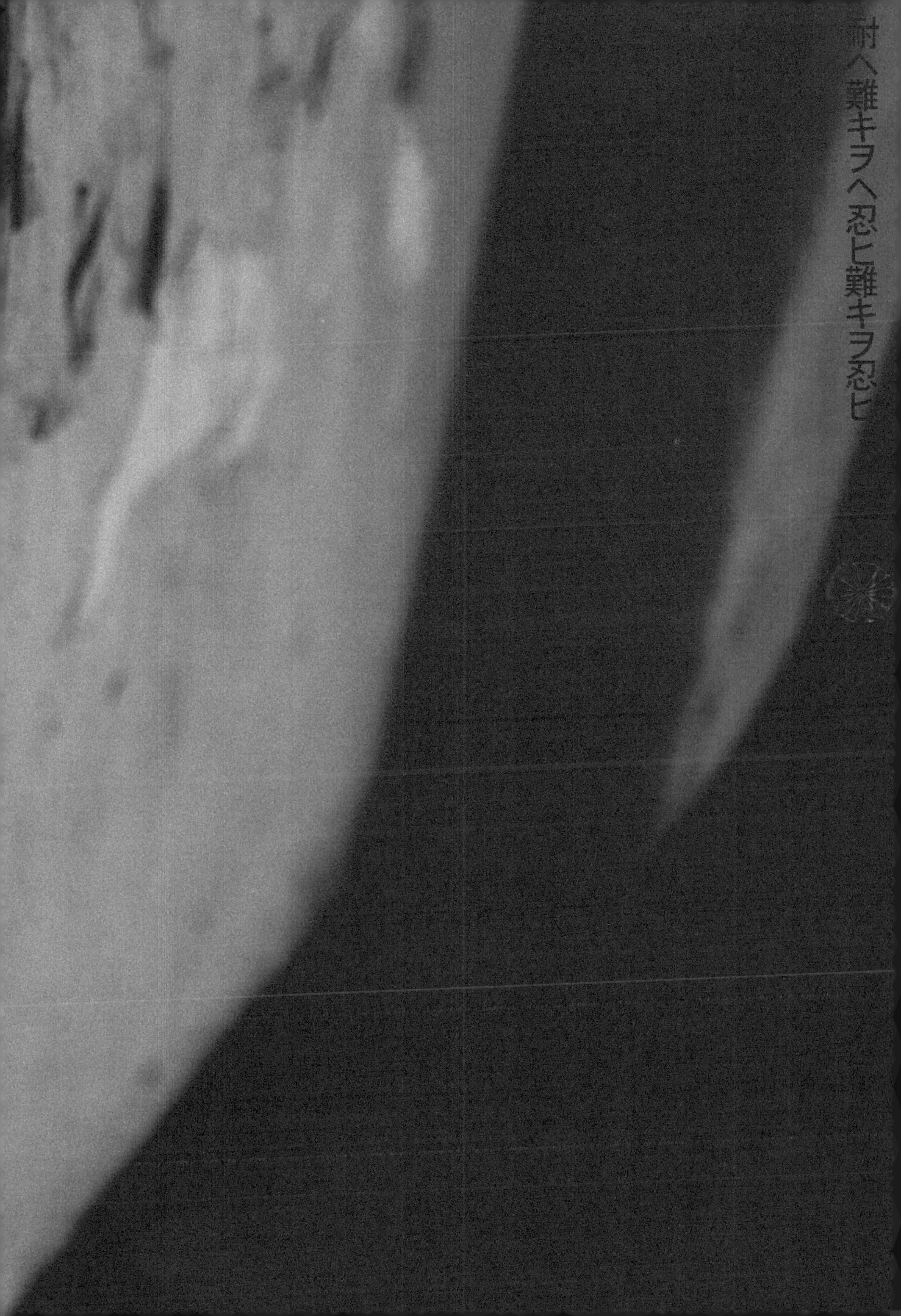

耐ヘ難キヲヘ忍ヒ難キヲ忍ヒ

耐ヘ難キヲヘ忍キヲ忍ヒ

Punch in, tune out

-I wonder if people are going to remember us?
-What, when we're dead?
-Yeah.
-Well I think people will talk about how you changed the world.
-I wonder what they'll say about you, in your obituary. I like that word.

-Nothing nice, I don't think.

-- *George Hickenlooper (dir.),* <u>Factory Girl</u>

What do we do when we attend to the notion of creating,
producing and – generally – making things up? Enterprises and
factoring practices that pertain to the commercial history of a
life – of collective lives – are the tangible effects of the human
imagination put to work, to real creative ends. Often, artists stand
at a threshold at odds with such certainties as affirmative, and rely
on the commoditising effects of the human productive impulse.
The challenge for the artist, for the poetic soul, is to embrace this
as one that is as real, and as fulfilling as any other.

The simultaneously cumulative and separate acts of creating, of
constructing, and of making are not only acts of fictionalising, they
are also acts of completion, unceasingly bound to respond one
to another, all with a mind of keeping alert against re-fabricating
the unmakeable, as well as the unmade. This can only be done,
<u>Requiem for the Factory</u> argues, by all the while insisting on the
otherness of the other.

> She longed for another adversary;
> something to pit herself against—learn its moves, strategies,
> techniques; spar, train, hurl herself into constant battle.

This is achieved with the tacit complicity with the fact that the
act brings attention to the unavoidable truth of selectivity, that
acts of remembrance become narrowed into exclusive, excluding
impulses.

<u>Requiem for the Factory</u> considers these inherent conflicts of
the creative heart through those extended tropes of systematic,
structured modes of production – observing the possible
underlying differences that lie within the word's connotative
implications, indeed structures it – by way of the manner in
which it can be conducted through various levels of an extended
narrative.

> She often remembered that her only hope lay in forgetting.
> Not just of the time that was, or even of time itself, but the
> forgetting that memory itself brings.
> Perhaps this is how hope works—

Making, we are reminded, is premised upon memory (remembrance, recollection), the shadow of amnesia upon which is always
and already cast – the unbreakable ties between forgetting and
remembering latch themselves on the past more than they do the
present. And if nostalgia has a say in the thing, the imaginative
return can quite easily be mistaken for an attempt to remember
in order to fabricate; an attempt, in other words, to dehumanise,
deny the one thing that confirms absolute mechanisation. As if
thinking has anything to do with it.

The impetus that drives this narrative is tightly woven into the
texture that clothes a notional entity whose cultural and social
raison d'être it is to perform the role of a highly-functional conduit
between source and consumption.

Material-dependent, the setting is neither brick nor mortar by any stretch of the imagination, but rather – in the trajectory of design and contemplative practice – an extension of repetition, of the same and always the same.

> Time used to bother her more than
> anything else; after all, her space was fixed,
> determined, set by a schedule, routine; time.
>
> Punching out was her ticket to
> freedom.

As this role is treated in <u>Requiem for the Factory</u>, the ideas of the repeat, routine, and return take on a heightened position in the narrative of transience, movements, speculation, submission, control, and other assorted significations that reinforce the inventiveness of both the physical and emotional space that is the sense of self.

The book further takes the act of making to absolute, almost absurd, ends by constantly returning to the idea of timeliness, playing even its central voice as time-keeper *par excellence* to a kind of quartz-like precision.

> There was a time when she would have told me her
> thoughts, her dreams, her memories—can someone tell
> you other than their memories; when they tell you, does it

become a future possibility?
That might have been the reason she used to tell me so
much—her distaste of time.

Indeed, time, that most profound of units of production,
is a central figure in the book which, if read alongside the
accompanying, hypnotic images, can offer us a portrait of the
manner in which the various narrative concerns that construct a
factory of remembrance can be deployed to brilliant artistic ends.
And in the portrayal here, it is possible to read <u>Requiem for the
Factory</u> as an un-ideological reply to the materialist imaginary. It
plays ideological critical gestures at their own game.

Lim Lee Ching
October 2012
Singapore

Jeremy Fernando is the Jean Baudrillard Fellow at the European Graduate School, where he is also a Reader in Contemporary Literature & Thought; and a Fellow of Tembusu College at the National University of Singapore. He works in the intersections of literature, philosophy, and the media; and has written 5 books—most recently, <u>Writing Death</u>. Exploring his thinking through other media has led him to film, music, and art; and his work has been shown in Seoul, Vienna, Hong Kong, and Singapore. He is the editor of the thematic magazine <u>One Imperative</u>.

Kenny Png is a multi-disciplinary creative who built his
foundation on producing, directing, and writing hours of factual
content for broadcasters including National Geographic,
Discovery, and History Channel among many others. In his search
for the perfect story, he has left his boot print in over 80 cities
across nearly 30 countries.

Apart from documentary film-making, his other passion is music;
and he has played for many pioneering Singaporean bands
including Meltgsnow, In Each Hand A Cutlass, as well as the city's
first Chinese gothic punk band, La' Dies.

More recently, he has turned his attention to the past with
the founding of singaporestoreroom.com; an online museum
dedicated to preserving the memory of the mundane on the island
of Singapore.

Yanyun Chen is a nomadic *gun-for-hire*. Her interest lies
in animation, illustration, design, typography, games, and
miniature set building. She is studying philosophy and media at
the European Graduate School, and is an atelier student at the
Florence Academy of Art, with a BFA (first class) in animation
from Nanyang Technological University, and has attended
The Animation Workshop in Denmark and Puppetry in Prague
programmes.

She works under the artist name Piplatchka, and Stick and
Balloon, and her clients include IDEO, National University of
Singapore, Audi, Vickers Ventures, and Studio Soi.

Lim Lee Ching teaches at the SIM University, Singapore. His research interests include: literary Englishes, Modernism and violence, literary aesthetics, the Canon, non-ideological cultural theories, and language and the oral tradition. He is the editor of Peter van de Kamp's poetry collection <u>Scratch & Sniff</u> (2010).

ne is photographable, 'photogenic', and this is perhaps the catastrophe, that one can be photographable, that one can be captured and caught in time ..."

(Hubertus von Amelunxen; in conversation with Jacques Derrida and Michael Wetzel)